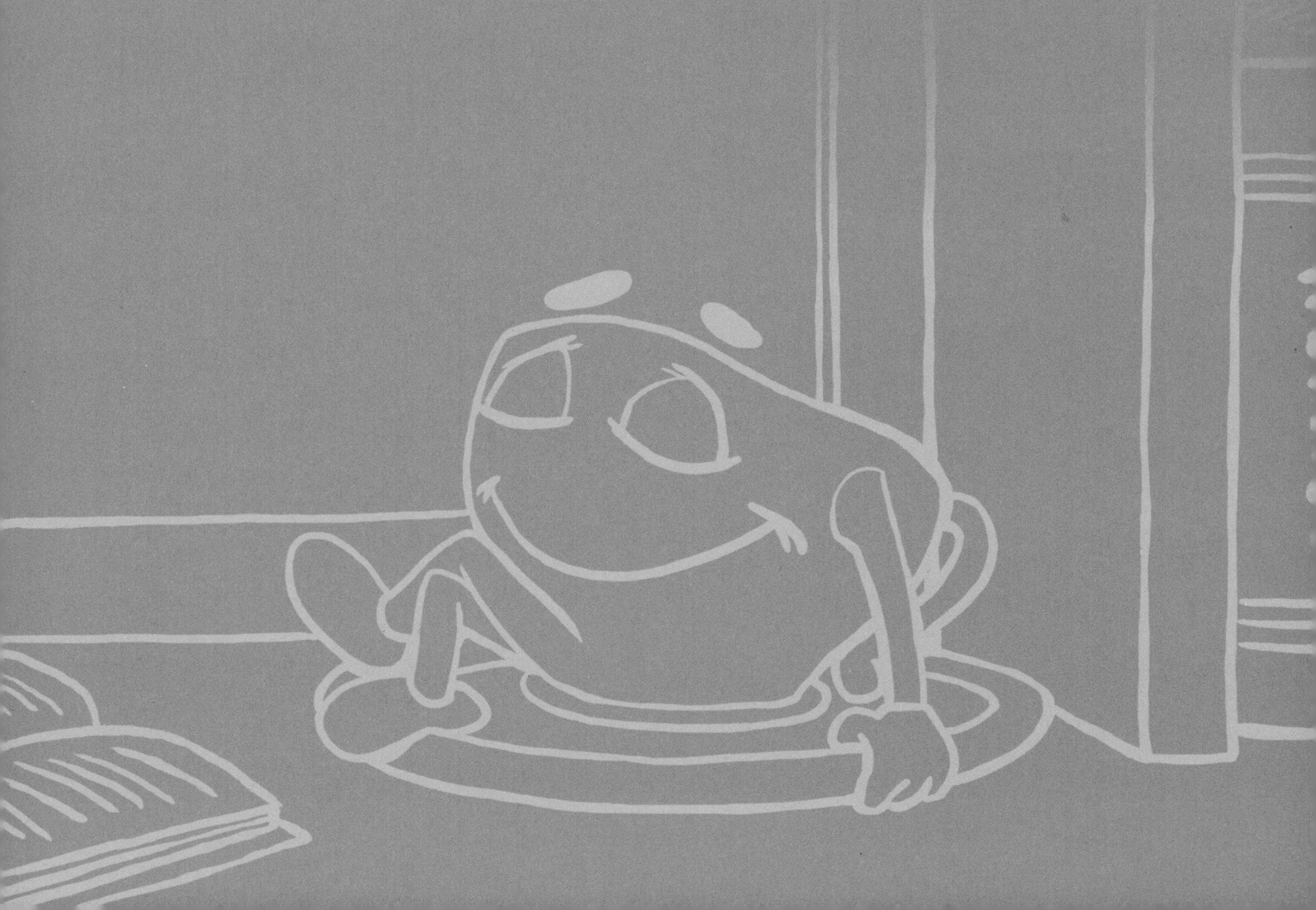

Charles T. Cup

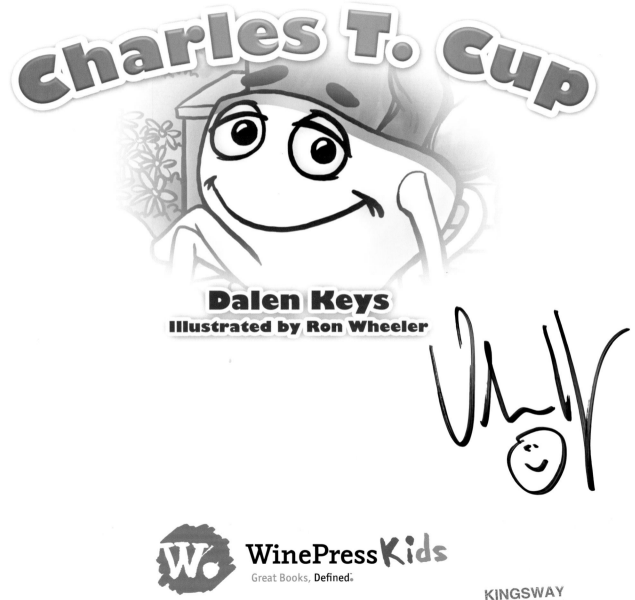

Dalen Keys
Illustrated by Ron Wheeler

WinePress Kids
Great Books, Defined.

WinePress Publishing (PO Box 428, Enumclaw, WA 98022) functions only as book publisher. As such, the ultimate design, content, editorial accuracy, and views expressed or implied in this work are those of the author.

ISBN 13: 978-1-60615-174-7
ISBN 10: 1-60615-174-6
Library of Congress Catalog Card Number: 2011924915

To:
Jonathan and Kim,
Tom, Janice and all my Friends at the Sunday Breakfast Mission,
Hannah, and Mitzie, of course!

Charles T. Cup gazed at himself in the mirror.

"My golden rim is so beautiful!" he said.

"I'm spectacular."

"I'm magnificent."

"I am absolutely marvelous!"

When guests were coming, Charles marched around like a general barking commands and snapping orders to the Others.

"What are you doing up here, you creepy Creamer?" roared Charles. "This is my place! I'm the star of this china cabinet. Get back there with the Others."

"Get into your places, you silly Saucers."

"Platters, stop that singing right now! We don't have time for that nonsense."

Charles always served the hot, creamy coffee to the powerful princes, the famous movie stars, and the best-selling authors.

Of course, Charles always glimmered a little brighter for guests.

"I looked soooooo fabulous today," said Charles loudly enough for everyone to hear.

He never noticed the ugly frowns and grimaces he got from the Others.

Sometimes, he sat leisurely in the library during afternoon tea, resting comfortably in his cozy saucer while basking in the warm sun.

Charles often soaked in bubbly baths.
However, it was during one such bath
when tragedy struck.

One night, as Charles climbed out of a lovely warm bath, there came a loud,

CLACK! CLANK! CRACK!

"Ouch! You big clumsy oaf!" he screamed at the Platter.

Charles' head swam and his ears rang.
He twisted and strained to see his
beautiful golden rim.

"Oh no, it can't be!" he gasped as he
saw the ugly nick on his rim. "That's real
gold. This can't be happening to me!"

Charles crept quietly into his place in the china cabinet hoping that no one would see him. But soon the Others started whispering and pointing.

"Who is that with the huge, ugly nick?" bellowed the Butter Dish.

"I think it's Charles," declared a Dinner Plate.

"No, no, no," said a sassy Salad Bowl. "I think you mean CHIP!"

Everyone burst into wild laughter—everyone except Charles.

Charles hung his head. "Can't they call me Charlie or Chuck? Anything but Chip!"

Later, when everyone finally quieted down, he noticed the Others were cracked and chipped too, but that didn't make him feel any better.

The next day, Mrs. People said, "We need a china set that's new and fresh. Let's get rid of this old one."

That very morning, Chip and all the Others were packed away in a dingy cardboard box. That afternoon, Mr. Driver loaded them into the car.

"Where are we going?" Chip wondered.

Some of the Others whimpered, some of the them cried, "Boo Hoo Hoo."

The car stopped suddenly, and Chip peeked out of the dark cardboard box and saw a little sign on a red brick building that simply said, THE MISSION.

The door slammed behind Mr. Driver as he stepped into The Mission and set the box, and Chip, on a table.

"Will you take this old china set for your thrift store?" said Mr. Driver. "I'm afraid it's kind of banged up."

A nice lady with red hair peeked inside the box. She picked up Chip and gently rubbed her soft finger over his nick and smiled sadly. "Of course, we will. Thank you very much."

Chip was placed on a shelf in The Mission's Thrift Shop, directly between a big superhero cup and some old plastic cereal bowls. Chip sobbed, "My beautiful life is over."

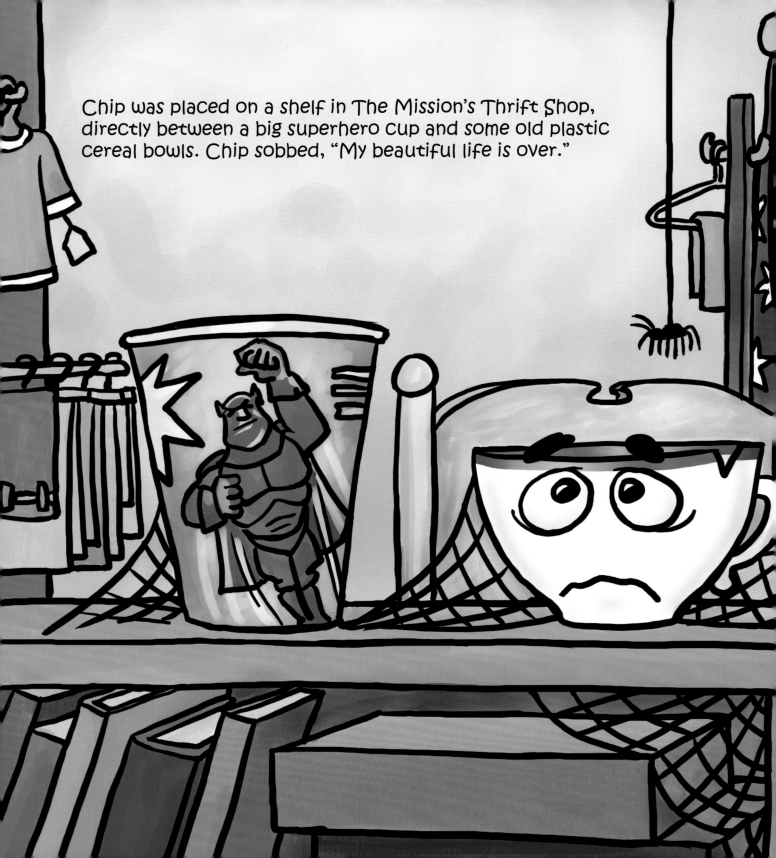

Days passed as Chip sat and sat on the shabby shelf with layers of dust slowly covering his rim of real gold. Occasionally, a curious spider crawled over him making him shiver.

Late one night, a person with rough hands carefully took Chip down from the shelf.

"I could use this little cup—chipped rim and all," said the Friendly Person. "You know, that rim might even be real gold. I'm going to call you Chip."

Somehow it sounded nice when the Friendly Person called him Chip. Chip smiled, just a little, for the first time in weeks.

"I'm glad I found you," said the Friendly Person as they left the Thrift Shop. "Let me show you our home."

Chip gasped as they immediately stepped into another room right there in the Mission. "Why aren't we leaving?" thought Chip as he looked around and saw men resting on neatly arranged beds or reading at desks.

"We live right here in the Mission," said the Friendly Person as he sat down on one of the beds and placed Chip carefully on a pillow beside him. "This is our special place. I know it's not much to look at, but it's warm and it's safe."

"We work here too," said the Friendly Person as he carefully wiped the layers of dust off Chip. "We help homeless people that feel unloved and unwanted. So many homeless people just need some clean water to drink or some hot coffee. You can help me serve them. We'll be a great team, you and I. Let's get some sleep because we'll be busy tomorrow. Goodnight, Chip."

"What?" thought Chip. "Are there really people that just need something to drink?"

The next day, Chip rode in a shopping cart perched proudly on top of a stack of blankets right next to the coffee and water containers.

Chip helped the Friendly Person serve cold water or hot coffee to anyone that needed a drink.

Sometimes the people were dirty.

Sometimes they smelled bad.

Sometimes they even looked scary to Chip.

But they were always happy to get a drink. No one even cared about his nicked rim.

Many days later, Chip thought about his old life as Charles T. Cup. No longer did he sit in the library and soak up the sun. Now, he listened to birds singing as he sat under a bright blue sky in a little park.

And that was spectacular!

No longer did he sleep in a beautiful China Cabinet. Now, he slept on a little bed at the Mission tightly nestled next to his Friendly Person.

And that was magnificent!

Now, Chip knew life was not about beauty, or gold, or even fame.

Instead, he understood life is about serving other people—even if you have a nick.

And best of all, Chip was loved for just being himself.

Chip snuggled comfortably into the caring hands of his Friendly Person. As his eyes slowly closed, a peaceful smile flashed across his face as he thought, "Life is now absolutely marvelous!"

Author's Note:

The Mission is based on The Sunday Breakfast Mission in Wilmington, Delaware that is reaching out to the homeless.

The Sunday Breakfast Mission provides Shelter for more than 165 homeless men and 120 women and children every night. There is a **Long-Term Discipleship Program** for 45 men and 40 women suffering from homelessness, addiction, and other major life problems (Chip's Friendly Person was in this Program). Over 200 men, women, and children receive a warm **Community Meal** every night. **Free clothing and furniture** are available for needy families through the community outreach program. The Sunday Breakfast Mission sponsors a **Back-to-School Rally** for over 2,000 boys, girls, and parents in which they provide encouragement, positive messages, and backpacks with school supplies. A **Career Education Center** gives hundreds of individuals an opportunity to learn to read, graduate from high school, and plan a new work life. And, finally, the **Thrift Store** gives families and individuals the opportunity to obtain critical goods otherwise unavailable because of cost (Chip was in this Thrift Store).

Sunday Breakfast Mission
P.O. Box 352
Wilmington, DE 19899

Phone: 1-877-748-7616

E-mail: info@sundaybreakfastmisson.org